ECHOES OF MISTY VALE.

(Tales of Mystery and Dread).

Vaishnavi Santhosh Kumar

Special thanks to the person who holds my surname.

CONTENTS

INTRODUCTION

"Into the Dark Shadows: Discovering Misty Vale Haunted Legacy."

In the middle of an ancient forest, where the trees stand tall and their branches interweave like skeletons dancing hands against the sky, remains a village almost forgotten.Misty Vale, as it is called by those who still dare to say its name, does not appear on any map or travel guide. It exists in whispers carried by the wind, in the conscious looks of peasants who are all too aware of the secrets that linger within its mist-shrouded boundaries.

The air in Misty Vale is thick with the weight of centuries-old tales of spectral figures seen at dusk, creepy lights dancing in the windows of long-abandoned houses, and an overpowering sense of anxiety that would settle like a blanket over every person who dares to walk through its narrow cobblestone streets after the sunset.

The village actually appears to be frozen in time; its architecture is an amalgam of inviting houses with thatched roofs and crumbling stone walls, revealing the scars of ancient rivalries and unspoken curses. Narrow lanes of twist and turn lead to hidden nooks where ghosts appear to gather, and each corner carries the promise of a secret beyond our comprehension.

Even though there are ghostly echobes and unsolved secrets, Misty Vale is more than just a place of evil and misery. It is a web integrated with the connections of generations who have lived there, each adding to the rich variety of mythology and the story that connects the village together.

Become part of me as we explore the darkest corners of Misty Vale, where the boundaries between fact and myth have been blurred and every stone holds a story screaming to be told. In the pages that follow,

we are going to uncover the secrets that existed beneath its surface, the truth behind its haunting profile, and sometimes we even see the spirits who still roam its endless streets.

Welcome to Misty Vale, a place where the past murmurs in the darkness and the souls of the ancestors linger just beyond our perception.

CHAPTER 1

"Ghosts of Misty Vale."

Misty Vale, wrapped among ancient trees and tangled vines, rises from the fog like a buried dream. Its cobblestone streets, worn smooth over generations, connect through a maze of charming houses with thatched roofs and crooked chimneys. Each home carries the footprints of time—crumbling walls covered by wind and rain, windows hung with cobwebs that sparkle in the pale moonlight.

The village square, an attraction of both life and myth, revolves around an ancient stone fountain. It was once a source of refreshment for weary travellers, but now it stands dry, its exquisite carvings surrounded by seaweed and mushrooms. Surrounding the area are cafes and restaurants where people assemble, chatting silently as if they don't want to disturb Misty vale's lingering silence.

Misty Vales switch at dawn as darkness spreads across cobblestone streets and the

sun's last rays evaporate behind the ocean. Lantern come to life, creating flickering patterns of light that dance across ancient stones. It is a time when the hurdle between the normal and supernatural realms dissolves, and people rush home, throwing anxious looks over them at ghost figures that appear to move under the darkness.

The Weeping Willow tree, which has a towering silhouette, is one of the village's prominent landmarks. Its sharp branches drop low, creating a veil of gloom over a small cemetery with ancient monuments falling at frightening angles. Tales warn of a miserable widow who haunts the tree's embrace, her spirits wandering in the mournful branches on dark evenings, her melancholy weeps calling through the silence.

Beyond the tree's reaches is murmuring Hollow, a peaceful meadow where flowering trees flourish, ignoring the village's gloomy

status. Even here, beneath the gentle fall of grass and the pleasant perfume of blossoms, there is a concealed funeral cemetery. Local mythology tells of restless spirits whose uttered secrets fly on the breeze, leaving their presence felt instead of seen by those who dare to wander too closely.

As evening falls, the people appear to hold their breath, awaiting the inevitable arrival of darkness. And it is then that Misty Vale reveals its true nature–a place where the past lingers in every darkness, where the ghosts of the deceased walk together with people who lived, and where stepping forward is an adventure into the unknown territory.

In the heart of Misty Vale, with its ageless streets and whispered myths, has the promise of discovery and the excitement of solving riddles that have lasted generations. Our adventure begins here, in this creepy village—a journey into the darkness, where every turn of

the page gets us closer to the truth hidden
behind Misty Vale's well-known history.

CHAPTER 2

"The Legend of the Weeping Willow."

In the heart of Misty Vale, with its ageless narrow streets and moaned rituals, lies the promise of exploration and the excitement of solving generations-old mysteries. Our quest begins here, in this haunted village—a journey into the darkness, where each turn of the page brings us closer to the truth hidden behind Misty Vale's well-known history.

According to local mythology, the Weeping Willow is more than just a tree; it is a symbol of agony and mourning. In the past, a young widow named Elza searched for peace beneath its branches and bark after losing her beloved husband in a tragic accident. Eaten by sadness and unable to find calm, she would visit the tree every night, her tear-streaked face emphasised by the moonlight.

As the weeks turned into months, people began to talk of weird incidents near the weeping trees. Some reported hearing quiet,

melancholy murmurs floating through the branches, while others saw a ghostly figure dressed in white moving in the tombstones with airy grace. Elza, they whispered, she had become one with the tree, her spirit permanently linked to its roots and branches.

On dark nights, when the curtain of darkness between the realms is thin, people brave enough to approach the Weeping Willow experience an overwhelming sense of melancholy in the air. Some believe they have heard Elza's voice, a sweet lament carried by the wind as she mourns the death of her beloved.

The people of Misty Vale, while aware of the tree's haunting presence, consider it with both love and horror. They leave bouquets and little gifts at its foot, hoping to calm the restless ghost that lives in its darkness. Children urge one another to approach its branches after dark, their hearts pumping with a mix of

fascination and fear.

Meanwhile, with the pain that sticks to the Weeping Willow, there is a fascinated beauty—a reminder of the ending power of love and loss, as well as the human spirit's determination in the face of tragedy. The tree stands as a quiet witness to the passage of time, its trunk and branches waving mournfully in the breeze, a melancholy warning that some stories are so deeply created in a place's essence that they become eternally connected to its identity.

As we wander deeper into Misty Vale, the mythical tale of the Weeping Willow serves as a haunting symbol of the village's struggling history and its dark secrets that anticipate those who are brave enough to seek them out. The next chapter of our adventure is waiting for us in the hidden corners of its branches, spoken by the wind—a voyage into the heart of a fable that will not be forgotten.

CHAPTER 3

"Murmurs of Whispering Hollow."

Whispering Hollow is located beyond Misty Vale village, where mist swirls around ancient trees and the fragrance of wildflowers hangs deep in the air. It is an oasis of quiet beauty and whispered murder mysteries

Whispering Hollow, hidden in an enchanting meadow, contrasts sharply with Misty Vale's gloomy reputation. Sunlight penetrates through the branches of towering trees, creating warm patches on the ground. Butterflies glide gently in the petals, their delicate wings gleaming out against the emerald leaves.

In spite of its appearance of sereneness, Whispering Hollow is not without its mysteries. According to local mythology, there is a hidden burial cemetery located within the heart of the meadow where the ghosts of the deceased might rest and the cover of darkness between the living and the dead disappears.

As dusk falls over Whispering Hollow, bringing mysterious figures across the grassy area, the atmosphere changes slowly. The air gets flooded with almost real energy, and some people who stroll here report strange sensations—a delicate touch of cool breeze against the skin, an immediate glance of movement at the corner of the eye, or the distant murmur of voices carried by the wind.

Visitors to Whispering Hollow frequently report feeling a deep sense of serenity and being connected to something beyond themselves. They talk about eras of wisdom and comprehension, as if the voices from the past are guiding them and revealing buried truths. Sceptics dismiss these events as creations of the imagination, but those who have felt the embrace by Whispering Hollow's mystical setting understand there is more to this calm meadow than what they see.

Stories linger about an evil spirit that watches over Whispering Hollow is a kind being supposed to help wandering souls find eternal rest and to console those who seek peace in the graves. Some believe to have seen a figure wrapped in mist strolling silently in the tombstones with a grace beyond explanation.

At the heart of Whispering Hollow is a sense of eternity, a recognition that the ghosts of the dead continue to haunt the places they were familiar with and loved. It serves as a reminder that death is not the final chapter but rather a transition—a journey into the unexplored, where echoes from the past echo across eternity's streets.

As we stand among the wildflowers and listen to the soft flutter of leaves in the breeze, Whispering Hollow invites us to explore its hidden depths and uncover the secrets buried behind its quiet disguise. In the waning light of day, we embark on an exploration into the

heart of mystery and memory, led by the whispers of Whispering Hollow.

CHAPTER 4

"The Curse of the Abandoned Mill."

The traces of the abandoned mill stand high on a rough cliff overlooking Misty Vale, where the wind roars through the crooked branches and the cries of circling crows tear the sky—a melancholy witness to a tragic history that is carving itself into the village's bricks.

The mill, once a flourishing industrial hub, is where every turn of the page gets us closer to the truth hidden behind Misty Vale's well-known history.now in ruins, its spotted timbers and breaking walls bearing witness to a disaster that forever changed Misty Vale's fate. Local tales speak in hushed tones about a curse that visited the mill, a possessed energy unleashed by a sequence of tragic events that occurred within its gloomy walls.

It is told that ages ago, during the peak of Misty Vale's prosperity, the mill was the village's lifeblood—a place where grain was ground into flour and the rhythmic hum of machinery could

be heard throughout the surrounding hills. Families rely on its operations for their survival, and the mill's towering appearance dominates the village's skyline.

But prosperity can be temporary, and the mill's fortunes took an unfortunate turn one horrible night. Histories vary, but most agree that a violent storm blew through Misty Vale, pouring heavy rains that caused the nearby river to swell and surge. The mill, situated dangerously close to the water's edge, was unable to withstand the force of the floodwaters, and its foundations collapsed under the surge.

The mill workers were trapped within its walls, with their cries for help drowned out by the smashing storm. Villagers gathered on the cliffs above, helpless as the tragedy happened below. By the morning light, the mill was in ruins, its equipment inactive, and its halls screaming with the memories of lives lost too soon.

In the events of the tragedy, tales of a curse spread across Misty Vale. Some said that the mill was set up on sacred land, disturbing ancient spirits who had long lived on earth. Others described a furious ghost, the spirit of a mill worker who had died in the flood and was now haunting the buildings, seeking vengeance for the lives lost.

Regardless of its origins, the curse of the abandoned mill left a shadow over Misty Vale. The people avoided the worsening tower, fearing restless spirits claimed to roam its halls and terrible energy entering from its breaking down walls. Tales of weird phenomena—disembodied voices echoing through the night, flickering lights dancing in the windows, and freezing blows of wind that seemed to come out of nowhere—only added to the village's belief in the curse.

Today, the abandoned mill stands as a silent warrior over Misty Vale, a reminder of the

weakness of prosperity and the eternal force of mythology. Its collapsing building stands as a warning to those who dare to experiment with forces beyond their knowledge, and its sad past continues to haunt the village's subconscious.

As we gaze at the mill bones, we are reminded that Misty Vale's history is as wild as the storm-lashed cliffs on which it stops. The curse of the abandoned mill is a tribute to the village's strength in the face of misfortune and a heartbreaking warning that some wounds, like the scars engraved in stone, never truly heal.

CHAPTER 5

"The Ghostly Guardian of
Whitethorn Manor."

Whitethorn Manor.

48

Standing on the outskirts of Misty Vale, when the shadows fall and the forest begins to recover the land is the frightening shape of Whitethorn Manor—evidence of money, power, and a darkness that dwells behind its gates.

The manor, with its towering chimneys and ivy-clad walls, provide an impressive view of the village below. Once a majestic house owned by the mysterious Lord Whitethorn, it now stands in haunting solitude, its windows shuttered up, and its once-luxurious gardens covered with tangled weeds.

Rumour has it that Lord Whitethorn is a character soaked in mystery, with whispered tales of scandals and intrigues. Rumours of his wealth and power are only matched by tales of his illicit behaviour and the tragic destiny of his family within the manor's luxurious halls.

One of the most disturbing of these stories is about the manor's ghost guardian, a

ghostly figure that is claimed to patrol the grounds with fierce watch. Dressed in outdated clothing that moves quietly with each step, the spirit is said to represent Lord Whitethorn's restless soul, eternally bound to protect his ancestral castle from invaders and those trying to learn its deepest secrets.

Those who have visited Whitethorn Manor report feeling an overwhelming sense of foreboding—a physical heaviness that hangs in the air like suffocating clothing. Ghosts dance behind curtained windows, and the moonlight creates twisted figures on the breaking stone top, creating murmurs of unknown eyes gazing from within.

Local myth warns against visiting the manor after dark, when the ghostly guardian seems to be most active. Visitors report hearing ghost footsteps echoing down empty halls, doors that open and close on their own, and cold breaths of wind that appear to deliver voices from a different era.

Despite the tales of haunting and sadness, some believe that Whitethorn Manor contains secrets waiting to be discovered hidden chambers filled with lost treasures, ancient manuscripts describing Misty Vale's history, and clues that may reveal the mysteries that wrap the village in darkness.

As we stand before the hefty gates of Whitethorn Manor, its ivy-clad walls screaming centuries of secrets, we are dragged deeper into Misty Vale's mystery. The ghostly guardian stands as a silent guardian, a monument to the lasting power of history and the constant hunger for truth in the face of haunting rivalry.

In the second phase of our journey, we will dig deeper into the mysteries of Whitethorn Manor's darkened streets, finding secrets that have remained inactive for decades and meeting the ghostly guardian that keeps watch over Misty Vale's deepest secrets.

CHAPTER 6

"Unravelling the Mysteries."

As darkness falls over Misty Vale, throwing long shadows across its cobblestone roads and ancient houses, the small town appears to hold its breath, anticipating the mysteries that wait behind its hidden corners. Among stories of ghostly encounters and spirit guardians, a tenacious few are drawn to discover the truths that have escaped both the curious and the cautious.

Misty Vale's excitement comes from its enigmatic tapestry of traditions and mythology, which have been passed down through centuries and are woven with threads of mystery and suspense. Among these stories, the haunted village's standing as a beehive of ghostly incidents and mysterious events continues to attract those who dare explore beyond the ordinary.

For others, Misty Vale is a place of haunting murmurs and restless spirits—a realm where the route between the living and the

dead bends and the echoes of centuries-old tragedies stick across time. The Weeping Willow tree stands as a gloomy monument to lost love and everlasting regret, its branches waving mournfully in the breeze, as if haunted by the soul of the mourning widow who found comfort beneath its branches and bark.

Whispering Hollow invites with its tranquil beauty and whispered secrets, where the subtle flutter of leaves and the soft murmur of unseen voices reveal glimpses into a world beyond mortal comprehension. Visitors may experience moments of clarity and connection here, surrounded by wildflowers and the soft glow of twilight, as if the ghosts of the deceased are guiding them to hidden truths.

The cursed elements of the abandoned mill stand witness to Misty Vale's stormy history; their cracking walls and echoing chambers are an unforgettable reminder of the village's determination in the face of tragedy, as

well as the lasting power of legend. The ghostly guardian of Whitethorn Manor, hidden in shadow and mystery, watches over its breaking building with fierce activity, a spirit guardian tasked with keeping its deepest secrets hidden from strangers.

As we venture deeper into Misty Vale, guided by curiosity and courage, we discover that the village's haunted reputation is more than just a collection of ghost stories and superstitions. It is a tapestry of human experience, a reflection of love and loss, success and tragedy, and the never-ending quest for knowledge in the face of scepticism.

Misty Vale reveals itself as a place where the past and the present intersect, where echoes of history bounce through the cobblestone streets and ancient walls. It is a population covered in mystery and darkness, and every journey ahead takes us closer to discovering the secrets hidden beneath its mythical surface.

As we prepare to embark on the final leg of our journey through Misty Vale, we are on the verge of discovery—a journey into the heart of a haunted village where every scream holds a story waiting to be told and the spirits of the past wait for our arrival with whispers of truth and rebirth.

CONCLUSION

"Echoes of Misty Vale."

In the serene harmony of dusk, as Misty Vale disappears into the embrace of shadows and the final echoes of whispered tales fade into the night, we reflect on our journey through this haunting village. Misty Vale has left an everlasting impact on our hearts and thoughts, from the cobblestone streets to the ancient cottages, the mysterious figures that haunt its dark corners, and the myths that tie its mythical past.

Our journey through Misty Vale has been one of discovery, as we strive to understand the mysteries concealed underneath its foggy veil. We have heard the melancholy murmurs of the Weeping Willow tree, where the ghost of a grieving widow remains among its mournful branches, eternally tied by love and loss. In Whispering Hollow, with the peaceful beauty of wildflowers and the gentle flutter of leaves, we have felt the temporary presence of restless spirits and the lingering whispers of lost secrets.

The cursed fragments of the abandoned mill are a monument to Misty Vale's determination in the face of disaster, serving as a harsh reminder of the village's stormy past and the continuing power of mythology. And at Whitethorn Manor, where shadows dance behind curtained windows and a ghostly guardian watches over its crumbling building, we gain a look into the mystery behind Lord Whitethorn and his family's awful fate.

As we stand at the crossroads of revelation and reflection, we are reminded that Misty Vale is more than simply a haunted and scary place. It is a tapestry made up of strands from human experience—a reflection of love and sorrow, victory and tragedy that go beyond time and location. Each cobblestone and ancient wall contains a narrative waiting to be told, and each contact with its spiritual inhabitants adds to our comprehension of the constant fascination of mystery and the timeless quest truth in the face of the unknown.

As the sun sets and Misty Vale slips into darkness, we carry the echoes of its ghostly legacy—a monument to the power of narrative and the human spirit's determination. Our journey through this ghostly village has been one of discovery and self-analysis, a reminder that the past whispers in the shadows and the souls of the dead linger just beyond our perception.

When we say goodbye to Misty Vale, we leave behind a place where the line between the living and the dead is thin, stories bleed into reality, and each step forward is a journey into the heart of mystery and memory. Though our time in this haunted enclave may come to an end, the echoes of Misty Vale's ghostly heritage will live on in our hearts—a monument to the eternal power of tale and the timeless quest for understanding in a world where truth and legend coexist.

As we leave Misty Vale, our hearts heavy with the weight of its haunting tales and bittersweet discoveries, we carry with us the knowledge that our journey through this haunted village has not only deepened our understanding of its mysteries but also illuminated the everlasting impact of narration and the timeless quest for truth in the face of uncertainty.

Farewell to Misty Vale,May your echoes linger on in our minds as a tribute to the enduring fascination of mystery, the power of the human spirit, and the never-ending quest to find meaning in a world where fact and mythology live together.

EPILOGUE

"Reflections on Misty Vale."

"Reflections on Misty Vale."

As we say goodbye to Misty Vale, its frightening stories and heartbreaking truths remain in our hearts. These mysterious and myth-filled people have shed light on universal issues such as love, sorrow, and survival. Beyond its cobblestone streets and historic cottages, Misty Vale is a reminder of the common desire for connection and understanding.

The journey through this haunting village has increased our admiration for storytelling's ability to.influence perceptions and connect us to the past. As we travel beyond Misty Vale's mist-shrouded borders, we decide to take with us the echoes of its stories—a tribute to the enduring excitement of mystery and the human spirit's tenacity in the face of mystery.

In waving farewell, we embrace Misty Vale's experiences and continue its heritage of research and discovery. May its echoes continue to inspire us as we embark on our own journeys, seeking truth and enlightenment in the darkness that hangs ahead.

About the Author.

On June 12, 1998, Vaishnavi Santhosh Kumar was born in Sivaganga, Tamil Nadu. She is a graduate in both fashion design and English literature. In 2023, she wed Santhosh Kumar, the love of her life. Her debut fiction story, "Echoes of Misty Vale," delves into the enigma at the center of Misty Vale and tells a tragic yet triumphant story of love and loss. Vaishu extends an invitation to readers to explore its supernatural mysteries and unravel the truth buried under the skin.

NOTES.

NOTES.

NOTES.

NOTES.